Felicia Bond

Poinsettia
and the
Firefighters

SCHOLASTIC INC.
New York Toronto London Auckland Sydney
Mexico City New Delhi Hong Kong Buenos Aires

ISBN 0-439-66194-3

12 11 10 9 8 7 6 5 4 3 2 1   4 5 6 7 8 9/0

Printed in the U.S.A.   23

First Scholastic printing, September 2004

To 132 Pondfield Road West

One Saturday morning Poinsettia's father said, "Poinsettia, how would you like to have your own room? I fixed up the two rooms on the top floor, one just for you, and one just for Petunia."

Poinsettia could hardly believe her ears. That afternoon Julius and Pierre moved into her old room.

"I bet you'll be scared to sleep by yourself," Pierre snorted.

"I bet I won't," Poinsettia said.

"You can have my favorite night-light," offered Chick Pea.

"No," Poinsettia grunted. "Only babies sleep with night-lights."

Poinsettia loved her new room. She admired it all evening and into the night.

Finally her father had to call up the stairs. "Turn out your light, Poinsettia," he said. "It's way past your bedtime."

"I can't even see my hoof in front of my face," Poinsettia thought.

She opened the curtains, but there was no moonlight or starlight. One by one the neighbors' lights went out.

Poinsettia's mother and father turned off their
light too. The night was very dark.
Suddenly something went CLANK!

"Petunia!" Poinsettia shouted.

"That was only your radiator," mumbled Petunia.

"I didn't see a radiator," Poinsettia said. "Are you sure I have one?" CLANK! went the sound.

"Let's invent a secret code," Poinsettia said. "If we hear a scary noise, I'll say 'peep' to make sure you're awake. Then you tell me what the noise is, okay?"

"Okay," said Petunia.

Poinsettia went back to bed.

Something creaked, v-e-r-y slowly. "Peep!" said Poinsettia.

"The stairs," said Petunia.

Something scratched, v-e-r-y roughly. "Peep!" said Poinsettia.

"A branch," said Petunia.

Something thumped, very loudly. "Peep!" said
Poinsettia. "Peep! Peep! ... PEEP!"

Petunia was asleep.

"Oh, no!" Poinsettia whispered. "I am the only
one awake."

She thought about the thump and the dark
places where it might be.

The thump came again, and it seemed louder
and closer than before. Poinsettia closed her eyes.
"Please let it be morning," she wished.

When she opened her eyes, there was a light outside.

It was pink and gold.

"The sun!" Poinsettia said.

The light got bigger and brighter. But it was not sunrise.

It was a fire on the telephone wire in front of Poinsettia's house.

"MOM!" Poinsettia shouted. "MOM! DAD!"

Poinsettia's mother called the fire department,

and the entire family watched the firefighters put
out the flames.

Afterward, three of the firefighters came into the house and filled out their report.

"You have a keen eye," one of them said to Poinsettia.

"Did the alarm wake you up?" Poinsettia asked.

"Oh, no," said the firefighter. "I'm the night watchman. I stay awake all night."

"I'm a night watcher too," Poinsettia said.

The firefighters waved good-bye.

Poinsettia went back to her room and looked out the window. The night was still dark.

Then Poinsettia saw it was not quite as dark as before.

Shining through the trees was the light from the
fire station six blocks away.

"I am not the only one awake," Poinsettia said.